Maria Espluga

I AM A FARMER

For my grandparents

Published in 2009 by Windmill Books, LLC
303 Park Avenue South, Suite # 1280, New York, NY 10010-3657

Publisher Cataloging Data

Espluga, Maria
      I am a farmer / by Maria Espluga ; translated by M. Rudo.
            p.   cm. – (I am a--)
      Summary: A child imagines the joys of being a farmer, including taking the cow out to pasture and growing a garden.
      ISBN 978-1-60754-248-3 – ISBN 978-1-60754-249-0 (pbk.)
ISBN 978-1-60754-250-6
      1. Farmers—Juvenile fiction   2. Imagination—Juvenile fiction   3. Farm life—Juvenile fiction   [1. Farm life—Fiction
2. Imagination—Fiction]   I. Title   II. Series
      [E]—dc22

Printed in the United States of America

an imprint of

WINDMILL
BOOKS
New York

I want to be a farmer.
I like to work on the land.

Early in the morning, I walk in the meadow, at least until winter comes.

I love the smell of the fields
after we have plowed them.

Spring comes and I am as happy as a bird!

I have a garden with a thousand colors,
tomatoes, peas, and pumpkins.

I go up to ask for rain from my neighbor,
Big-Nose the Giant.

A long nap in summertime
is as delicious as strawberry pie.

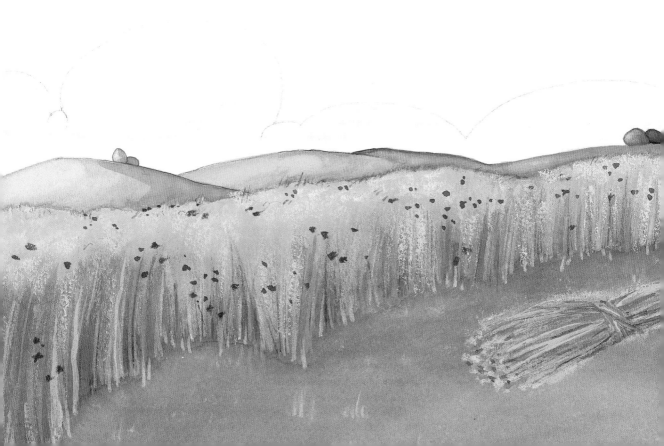

In autumn, the wind sings
and the leaves dance.

How cozy it is at home
when it's cold in the mountains!

I listen to the fire crackling at night,
when the elves and the fairies come out.

And before going off to bed . . .

A kiss and sweet dreams!